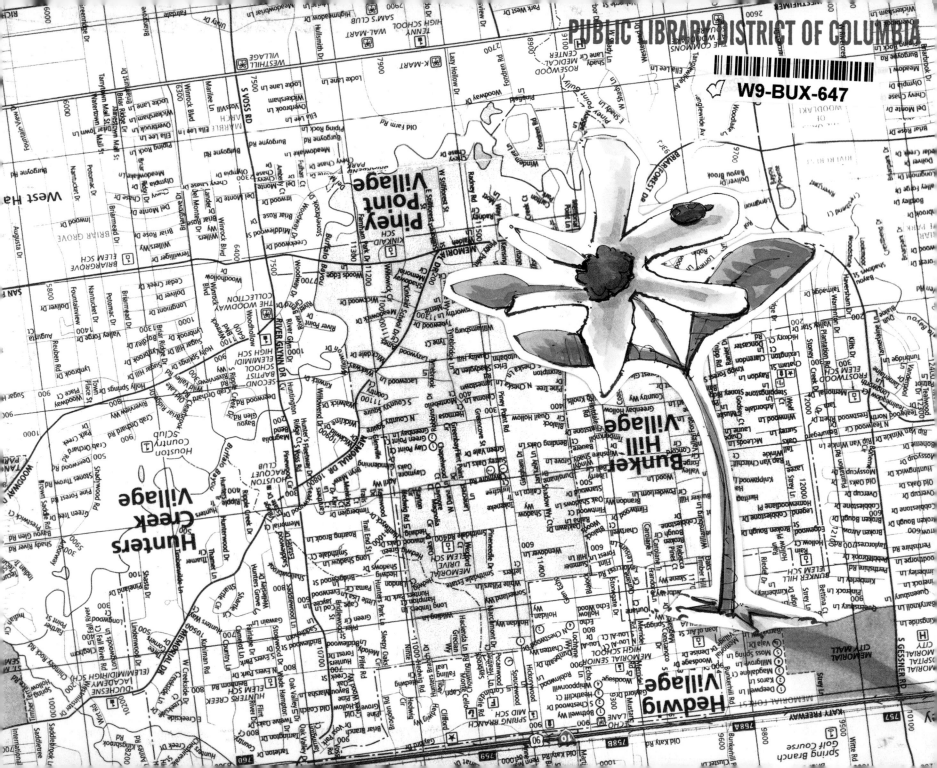

Treasure Map

BY Stuart J. Murphy

ILLUSTRATED BY Tricia Tusa

HarperCollins*Publishers*

LEVEL
3

To Aki and Kai—two real treasures
—S.J.M.

To Muffin and Amelia
—T.T.

The publisher and author would like to thank teachers
Patricia Chase, Phyllis Goldman, and Patrick Hopfensperger
for their help in making the math in MathStart® just right for kids.

HarperCollins®, ✿®, and MathStart® are registered trademarks of HarperCollins
Publishers. For more information about the MathStart series, write to
HarperCollins Children's Books, 1350 Avenue of the Americas, New York, NY 10019,
or visit our website at www.mathstartbooks.com.

Bugs incorporated in the MathStart series design were painted by Jon Buller.

Treasure Map
Text copyright © 2004 by Stuart J. Murphy
Illustrations copyright © 2004 by Tricia Tusa
Manufactured in China by South China Printing Company Ltd.

Library of Congress Cataloging-in-Publication Data
Murphy, Stuart J.
Treasure map / by Stuart J. Murphy ; illustrated by Tricia Tusa.—1st ed.
   p.   cm.
MathStart—Level 3, mapping
 Summary: An old map leads the members of the Elm Street Kids' Club to a buried time
capsule.
  ISBN 0-06-028036-0 — 0-06-446738-4 (pbk.)
  1. Map reading. [1. Map reading—Juvenile literature. 2. Buried
treasure. 3. Clubs.] I. Tusa, Tricia, ill.
GA130 .M87 2004
[912'.01'4]—dc22   2003017674
                                                                  CIP
                                                                   AC

Typography by Elynn Cohen   1 2 3 4 5 6 7 8 9 10   ❖   First Edition

Treasure Map

"Look what I found," yelled Matthew as he raced into the clubhouse. The members of the Elm Street Kids' Club all watched as he unrolled a big piece of paper.

"It's a treasure map," said Matthew.

"Treasure map! Treasure map!" repeated Petey, Meg's pet parrot, as everyone crowded closer to see.

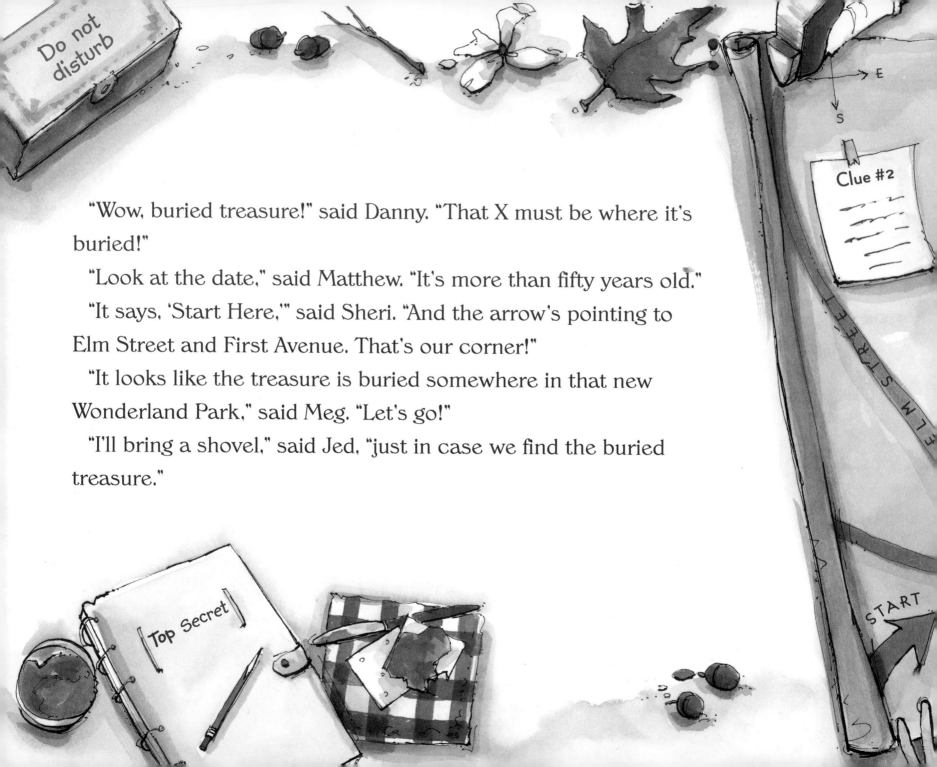

"Wow, buried treasure!" said Danny. "That X must be where it's buried!"

"Look at the date," said Matthew. "It's more than fifty years old."

"It says, 'Start Here,'" said Sheri. "And the arrow's pointing to Elm Street and First Avenue. That's our corner!"

"It looks like the treasure is buried somewhere in that new Wonderland Park," said Meg. "Let's go!"

"I'll bring a shovel," said Jed, "just in case we find the buried treasure."

They raced to the corner.

Then Matthew read Clue Number One:
"From Elm Street, walk down First Avenue toward
Rocky River. At the next corner, Oak Street, turn left."

"Rocky River's down that way," Jed said, pointing.

"Let's go," said Meg.

"Let's go! Let's go!" squawked Petey.

They turned onto First Avenue and marched toward Oak Street. Jed led the way.

Sheri put on her baseball cap and jumped behind Jed.

Danny followed, rubbing a new penny for good luck.

Meg shoved her comic book into her pocket and joined them.

And Matthew hurried behind with the map.

When they got to the corner of Oak Street
and First Avenue, they turned left.

"Here we are," said Jed. "And Wonderland
Park is over there. What's next?"

Buried

Clue #2

Now keep walking
about 125
giant steps until you
come to a dirt path
on the right that leads
to the park.

OAK STREET

Matthew read Clue
Number Two: "Now keep
walking about 125 giant steps
until you come to a dirt path on the
right that leads to the park."

"Gosh, that's a lot of steps," said Danny.

"Lot o' steps! Lot o' steps!"
chimed in Petey.

Treasure

DIRT

PATH

They counted 125 giant steps and looked to their right.

"There's no dirt path," said Danny, "but there's a big sidewalk."

"And it does lead to the park," said Meg.

"It looks like it's in the right place," said Jed, pointing to the map.

"Maybe it was a dirt path fifty years ago," said Sheri.

14

"We're getting closer," said Jed. "What do we do now?"
Matthew read Clue Number Three: "Walk up
the path through a pine grove and continue to the
top of the hill, where you'll find a big oak tree."

Sheri looked at the map. "Well, it looks like it's twice as far as it was from the corner to this sidewalk," she said. "That would make it 250 giant steps—all uphill."

"We can do it," said Jed.

"We can do it! We can do it!" agreed Petey.

While Jed counted off 250 giant steps, they passed through a group of pine trees and reached the top of the hill.

"I don't see any big tree here," said Danny as he sat down on an old stump.

"Me neither," said Jed. He picked up a newspaper from the ground and fanned himself with it.

"Wait a minute," said Sheri. "That stump was once a big tree. This could be the place after all."

Matthew looked at the map. "I think Sheri is right," he said.

19

"Okay," said Jed excitedly. "Now what?"

Matthew read Clue Number Four: "Cross Rocky River where you see a great big rock. Nearby, look for a flat rock with a big X on it. X marks the spot."

They started walking toward the river, and pretty soon they came to a big, moss-covered rock.

"This must be it," said Matthew, looking at the map to be sure.

Everyone started looking for a rock with an X on it. Everyone except Petey, that is. He just plopped himself down for a rest.

"C'mon, Petey," yelled Meg. "You can't stop now." She clapped her hands loudly behind his back.

Petey jumped up—and there it was! He had been sitting on a flat rock and Meg noticed a big X carved into the top.

"Petey found it!" Meg hollered. Petey ruffled his feathers proudly.

Jed could hardly wait. He grabbed his shovel and started
digging. Pretty soon he hit something that sounded like metal.

Jed reached in and carefully removed a flat metal box from the hole. It had been taped shut. He pulled off the tape and pried the cover open.

"Wow! Look at this cool old stuff," said Meg.

"It's a time capsule from another kids' club a long time ago," said Danny.

ELM STREET GAZETTE

JULY 9, 1950

Buy Now!

24

When they had finished looking at everything, Sheri asked, "Now what do we do with it all?"

"I know. Let's put it back for someone else to find," suggested Jed.

"Maybe we can add some stuff of our own and make it our time capsule too," said Matthew.

"Great idea!" said Meg.

"Great idea! Great idea!" chattered Petey.

"I'll put in my lucky penny," said Danny. "It's got this year's date on it."

"Well, I'll add my baseball cap," said Sheri, and in it went.

"Whoever finds it might like my comic book," said Meg.

"I'll add this newspaper," said Jed. "It has all of today's news in it."

Matthew pulled out a picture of the group that he carried in his pocket. He wrote "Elm Street Kids' Club" and the date on the back and tossed it in.

Petey grabbed a loose tail feather with his beak and put it right on top.

Super Dog

Jed closed the box and put it back in the hole. He covered it with dirt and carefully placed the rock with the X back on the top. "X marks the spot!" he announced.

As they started back to their clubhouse to hide the map, Petey squawked, "X marks the spot! X marks the spot!"

FOR ADULTS AND KIDS

In *Treasure Map,* the math concept is mapping. Decision-making skills, map-reading skills, and math concepts such as interpreting symbols and understanding direction and scale are included in this topic. These beginning skills lay the foundation for children to use and interpret larger and more intricate maps.

If you would like to have more fun with the math concepts presented in *Treasure Map,* here are a few suggestions:

- Prior to reading the story, read the title and ask the child to predict what will happen.

- As you read the story, refer to the map and help the child trace the path that the characters take to the buried treasure.

- Help the child make a map of his or her room. The map should include a key that contains symbols or pictures of the real items in the room. You might also consider making a map of the child's house, yard, or neighborhood.

- Reread the story. Point out the key on the map and discuss what the symbols mean. Find the river, the oak tree, and the other objects represented by the symbols.

Following are some activities that will help you extend the concepts presented in *Treasure Map* into a child's everyday life:

At the Mall: On your next trip to the mall, help the child first locate where he or she is on the mall directory map. Then help the child locate his or her favorite stores. Look at the key and discuss the meaning of the various symbols. Have the child find the nearest restroom and the nearest restaurant.

Internet: Visit a site on the Internet that maps directions. Help the child enter his or her address and that of a friend. Print the map and have the child trace the route from home to the friend's house. Does the map show the same route that the child would take? What things other than street names does the map show?

3-D Map: As a group project, make a three-dimensional map using clay and cardboard of a park near your home or school.

The following books include some of the same concepts that are presented in *Treasure Map*:

- MY MAP BOOK by Sara Fanelli
- MAPPING PENNY'S WORLD by Loreen Leedy
- X MARKS THE SPOT! by Lucille Recht Penner